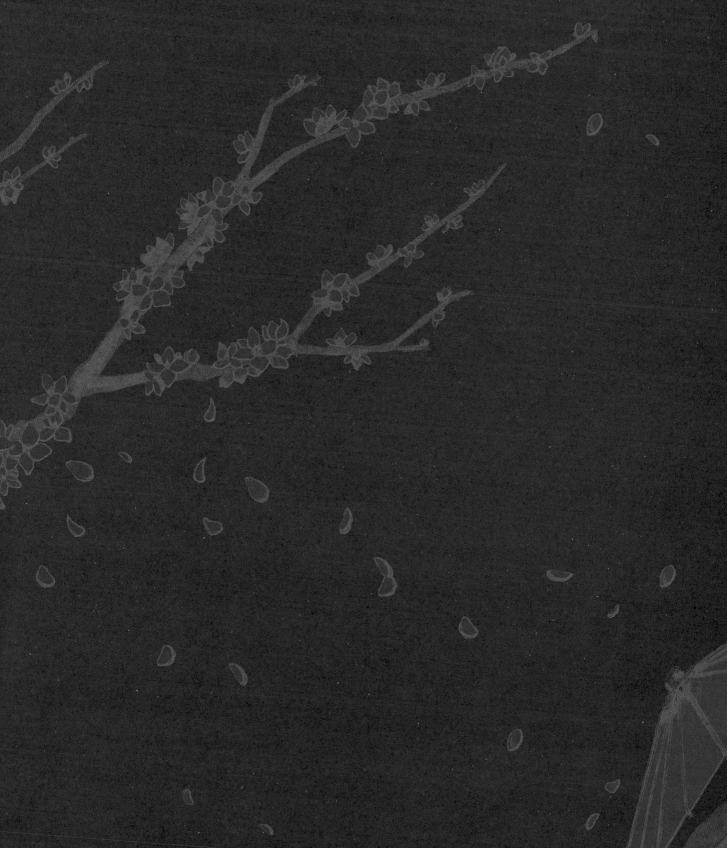

WOLF! WOLF!

To Spencer!
JOHN ROCCO

HYPERION BOOKS FOR CHILDREN
NEW YORK

For Aileen—you make my garden grow

Special thanks to Nami, Christine, and Brenda
for your wisdom and support

THE HUNGRY OLD WOLF was too slow to snatch birds and too stiff to chase rabbits, so he tried growing food in a small garden.

"Bah, weeds everywhere! There are so many I can't even find the vegetables." The old wolf growled, rubbing his empty stomach.

As he yanked dandelions from where his carrots should have been, his ears began to twitch.

WOLF'S
CARROTS

"WOLF! WOLF!"

The old wolf fumbled with his hearing aid.
Who's calling me? I don't remember having any friends on this mountain.

In fact, the old wolf didn't have any friends on any mountain.

"Maybe they have some food to share? A mere morsel would do," he said.

His bones creaked and his joints cracked as he slowly made his way toward the voice.

After a tiring climb and two stubbed toes, the old
wolf came to a clearing.

"What's this? A boy? With goats!" The old wolf
drooled with excitement. "Surely he can spare *one*
for a hungry wolf."

Before he could step into the meadow, a group
of villagers came clambering up the hillside.

The old wolf stayed hidden behind the bamboo as the villagers surrounded the boy.

"Where's the wolf?" a villager cried out, waving a stick.

"Did he take any goats?" another gasped.

"What wolf?" the boy giggled. "There is no wolf."

"We ran up this hill for *nothing*?" the eldest wheezed.

"Call us *only* if you see a wolf," scolded another.

The old wolf wasn't fond of angry villagers, especially ones with sticks, so he limped down to a nearby stream.

"Kids. Humph! Always playing tricks on old folks and old wolves." He groaned as he soaked his tired feet.

Before long the boy's cry came again.

"WOLF! WOLF! The wolf is taking the goats!"

Another wolf is taking those tasty goats?

The old wolf couldn't stand the thought and quickly hobbled back to the meadow.

The villagers were already there, huffing and puffing from running up the hill.

"Where is the wolf? Are the goats okay?" the villagers gasped.

"What wolf?" The boy laughed.

From behind a tree, the old wolf watched the villagers stagger back down the hill.

There's got to be a way to get one of those scrumptious goats from that trickster, he thought. Perhaps through a trick of my own.

The old wolf sat down to work out a plan and was soon snoring away and dreaming of mu shu goat and double-goat dumplings.

"WOLF! WOLF!" the boy yelled out again.

"Aaargh! I can't even enjoy the goats in my dreams! That boy is worse than weeds," the old wolf growled. He stretched his aching legs, and went to the meadow once more.

Perfect. Not a villager in sight.

The old wolf slowly crept out toward the boy. The goats swiftly scattered to the far edge of the meadow.

"Were you calling me over for lunch?" The old wolf grinned.

"WOLF! WOLF! There *is* a wolf!" the boy cried as he scrambled up a tree.

"Quit your yelling," said the wolf. "Those villagers won't believe you, anyway."

"But this time it's true, they have to believe me. You're a *real* wolf, and you're going to take the goats."

The old wolf knew his legs were too tired to chase down goats. He carefully lowered himself onto a nearby rock and gazed up at the boy. His lips curled in a smile.

"The villagers are only going to believe you if you really are missing a goat. I can help you with that." He grinned.

"Just one goat?" The boy leaned forward on the branch.

"I'm a picky eater. That plump one looks about right. But you have to bring it to me, because if I go over there, I might change my mind and grab them all."

"Bring it to you?" the boy asked.

"On the other side of the mountain," the old wolf said, "you'll find a small garden. Just tie it to the fence post there." And he started home.

The next morning the old wolf was overjoyed to see the plump goat nibbling away in his garden.

"Good fortune at last!" he said. "Today I'll feast like an old wolf should." He rubbed his paws together.

The wolf's mouth watered and his stomach grumbled as he crept up behind the goat. Suddenly he noticed something remarkable.

Everywhere he looked, there were ripe and juicy vegetables: baby bok choy, beautiful eggplant, ready-to-pick carrots, and even his favorite—onions. The old wolf couldn't believe his eyes.

Then he saw the goat happily eating the last few weeds. She saw him too, and froze in fear.

"You ate my weeds!" the old wolf said. "But why didn't you eat the vegetables?"

"Sorry, I'm a picky eater," she said. "Please don't eat me!"

The wolf looked at the plump goat and then at all the juicy vegetables, and back at the goat again. He sighed.

"Don't be sorry! You did my work for me. What's one breakfast compared to delicious vegetables for the rest of my days?"
The wolf smiled as he untied the goat.

"I could use a friend like you."
Plus, double-goat dumplings are overrated, anyway!